**'even the thousand-mile road
has a first step'**

"હજારો માઇલોની સફરની શરૂઆત માટે
એક ડગલું તો માંડવું જ પડે છે."

Milet Limited
Publishing & Distribution
PO Box 9916
London W14 OGS

First English-Gujarati dual language edition
published by Milet Limited in 1997

First English edition published in 1997
by Scholastic Limited, UK

Copyright © Helen Cowcher, 1997
Illustrations © Helen Cowcher, 1997

ISBN 1 84059 011 4

Printed in Turkey

The right of Helen Cowcher to be identified as the author and illustrator of this work has been
asserted by her in accordance with the Copyright, Designs and Patents Act, 1988.

JAGUAR

ચીત્તો

HELEN COWCHER

Gujarati translation by PRATIMA DAVE

MILET
LONDON

At dusk, a silent figure casts his gaze
forward and back across the lagoon.

સંધ્યા સમયે, એક મૂક ઓછાયો પાણીનાં સરોવરની આસપાસ,
આગળ અને પાછળ એમ ચોતરફ નજર નાખતો સરકે છે.

That same evening on the plain,
a rider making his way home,
sees marks left in the dust.

તે જ સાંજે મેદાનમાં, એક ઘોડેસવાર પોતાના ઘરે
પાછા વળતી વખતે ધૂળમાં પડેલા નિશાનો જૂએ છે.

In his mind he sees his herd.
He is worried. He's used to losing
cattle from sickness and drought.
But this is different.

તેનાં મન સમક્ષ પોતાના ઢોરોનું ધણ ખડું થઈ જાય છે.
તેને ચિંતા થવા લાગે છે. માંદગી અને દુકાળના કારણે પોતાના
ઢોરો ગુમાવવા માટે તે ટેવાયેલો છે. પરંતુ આ કંઈક જુદું જ છે.

His herd is under new threat from
an ancient foe, stalking his land,
but possessed of a mystical power
which holds sway over his thoughts.

તેનાં ઢોરોના ધણ ઉપર છુપાતા ફરતા જૂના દુશ્મનની
શિકારી નજર તોળાઈ રહી છે, પરંતુ તેનાં વિચારો પર
ગૂઢ શકિત છવાઈ જાય છે.

Very early next morning, he sets off
along the dry river bed,
stealthily searching
all the while.

બીજા દિવસે વહેલી સવારે, નદીના સુકાઈ
ગયેલા તટમાં ચોરીચૂપકીથી તે તપાસ કરવા
નીકળી પડે છે.

As the man walks, Jaguar swims
from his island hide-out.
Suddenly razor-sharp teeth pierce his tail.
Piranhas!
Biting and snapping!
Jaguar swims on, soon
escaping his tormentors.

માણસ શોધ કરતો રહે છે. એટલામાં ચીતો છૂપી
જગ્યામાંથી તરીને બહાર નીકળી આવે છે.
એકાએક, અસ્ત્રાની ધાર જેવા તીક્ષ્ણ દાંત તેના
લટકતા પૂંછડાને ચીરી નાખે છે.
તીક્ષ્ણ દાંતવાળી શિકારી માછલીઓ!
કરડતી અને બટકા ભરતી! ચીતો તેને પીડા
પહોંચાડનારાઓથી બચતો બચતો તરવાનું ચાલુ રાખે છે.

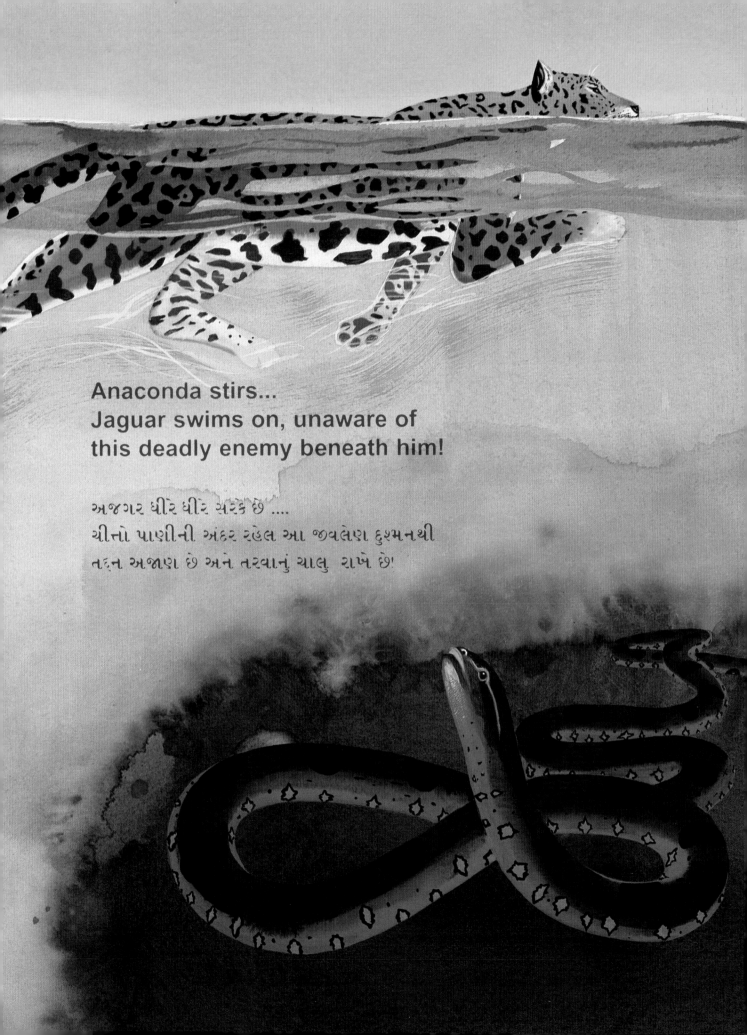

Anaconda stirs...
Jaguar swims on, unaware of
this deadly enemy beneath him!

અજગર ધીરે ધીરે સરકે છે ....
ચીત્તો પાણીની અંદર રહેલ આ જીવલેણ દુશ્મનથી
તદ્દન અજાણ છે અને તરવાનું ચાલુ રાખે છે'

On another shore, a basking caiman bares
his teeth, completely still.
As the day becomes hotter,
the man hunts in earnest,
soaking in signs with all his senses.

બીજા કિનારા ઉપર તડકાની મોજ માણતો મગર સહેજ પણ
અવાજ કર્યા વગર દાંતિયા કરે છે. દિવસ જેમ જેમ વધુ ગરમી
પકડે છે; તેમ તેમ શિકારી સુધબૂધ ખોઈને શિકાર કરે છે.

Quietly and carefully,
he follows Jaguar into the forest.

શાન્તિથી અને સાવધાનીથી, તે જંગલમાં
ચીનાનો પીછો પકડે છે.

Jaguar is also hunting.
Howler monkey sees him and
is frozen with fear!

ચીત્તો પણ શિકાર કરી રહ્યો છે.
હૂપ હૂપ કરતો વાંદરો ચીત્તાને જોઈને
ભયથી થીજી જાય છે!

He screeches desperately and
as if in a trance...

પછી જીવ ઉપર આવી જઈને ચિચિયારી કરવા
લાગે છે જાણે બાવરો ન હોય ....

...loses his grip
and tumbles to the ground.
Jaguar's search for food
is over for a while.

..... એટલામાં તે ઝાડ પરની પોતાની પકડ
ગુમાવી બેસતાં ઝાડ પરથી જમીન ઉપર પટકાઈ
પડે છે. થોડા વખત માટે, ચીત્તાની ખોરાક માટેની
શોધ પૂરી થાય છે.

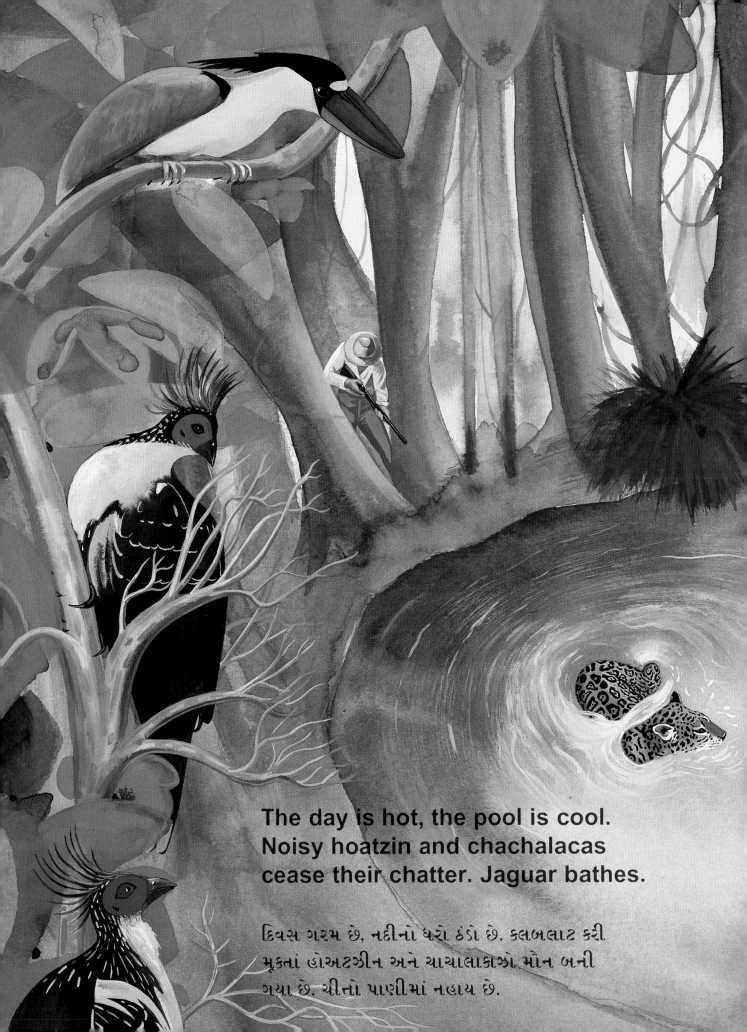

The day is hot, the pool is cool.
Noisy hoatzin and chachalacas
cease their chatter. Jaguar bathes.

દિવસ ગરમ છે, નદીનો ધરો ઠંડો છે. કલબલાટ કરી
મૂકતાં હોઅટઝીન અને ચાચાલાકાઝો મૌન બની
ગયા છે. ચીતો પાણીમાં નહાય છે.

As Jaguar relaxes his guard,
an eye is trained upon him.
The man's quest is over,
yet he feels uneasy.
It is rare for him to see
such a beautiful animal.

જેવો ચીતો થોડો અસાવધ બની જાય છે કે તરત જ
શિકારીની આંખ તેનાં ઉપર નિશાન તાકવા મંડાય છે.
શિકારની શોધ પૂરી થઈ ગઈ હોવા છતાં પણ માણસ
વ્યાકુળતા અનુભવે છે.
તેને આવા સુંદર પ્રાણીને નજીકથી જોવાની
બહુ ઓછી તક મળે છે.

The hunter holds his gun firm,
but his mind is troubled.
He fixes his sight and prepares
to fire but he cannot shoot.

શિકારી તેની બંદૂકને હાથમાં કસીને પકડે છે, પરંતુ
તેનું મન ઢચુપચુ છે.
શિકારી નિશાન તાકીને ગોળી છોડવા માટે તૈયારી
કરે છે પરંતુ ગોળી છોડી નથી શકતો.

Once, he recalls, our forests
and vast plains used to hide many
big cats and now there are few.
Against our dogs and guns they
stood no chance.
Their natural power counted for nothing!

It is as if the glade has cast
its spell upon him.

તેને યાદ આવે છે કે એક જમાનામાં આપણાં જંગલોમાં અને
ખુલ્લા મેદાનોમાં જંગી બિલાડા જેવા ઘણા પ્રાણીઓ વસતા હતા
પણ હવે અહીં થોડા જ બચ્યાં છે.
કુતરાઓ અને બંદૂકોની ગોળી સામે તેઓને બચવાની તક ન મળી.
તેમની કુદરતી શક્તિની ગણના કંઈજ ન થઈ!

જંગલની ખુલ્લી જગ્યાએ જાણે કે તેનાં ઉપર જાદુ કર્યું હતું.

Suddenly a vision flashes before him,
- a raging jaguar filling the air!
- an ancestral guardian protecting his own!

એકાએક તેની સામે એક સુંદર દૃશ્ય ખડું થયું,
- ક્રોધાવેશમાં ચીત્તાએ હવામાં છલાંગ ભરી!
- પુરાણો સંરક્ષક પોતાનાંઓની રક્ષા કરી રહો હતો!

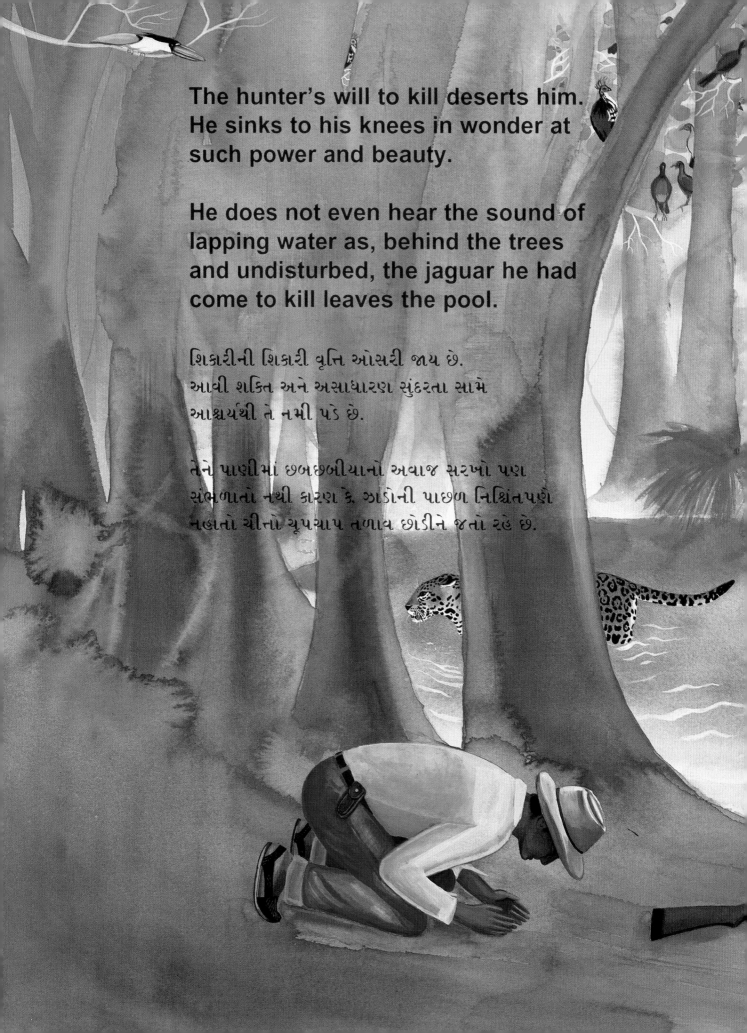

The hunter's will to kill deserts him. He sinks to his knees in wonder at such power and beauty.

He does not even hear the sound of lapping water as, behind the trees and undisturbed, the jaguar he had come to kill leaves the pool.

શિકારીની શિકારી વૃત્તિ ઓસરી જાય છે.
આવી શકિત અને અસાધારણ સુંદરતા સામે
આશ્ચર્યથી તે નમી પડે છે.

તેને પાણીમાં છબછબીયાનો અવાજ સરખો પણ
સંભળાતો નથી કારણ કે, ઝાડોની પાછળ નિશ્ચિંતપણે
નહાતો ચીતો ચૂપચાપ તળાવ છોડીને જતો રહે છે.

Scarlet macaws fly over the man as
he makes his way back through the forest.
He feels no regret.
His mind is full of his vision
and his heart has softened.

જંગલમાંથી થઈને ઘર પાછા વળતી વખતે રંગબેરંગી
પોપટો તેનાં માથા ઉપરથી પાંખો ફફડાવતા ઉડે છે.
તેને કોઇ જ અફસોસ નથી.
તેનું મન તેણે જોયેલા દૃશ્યથી ભરાઇ ગયું છે અને
હવે તેનું હૈયું મૃદુ થઇ ગયું છે.

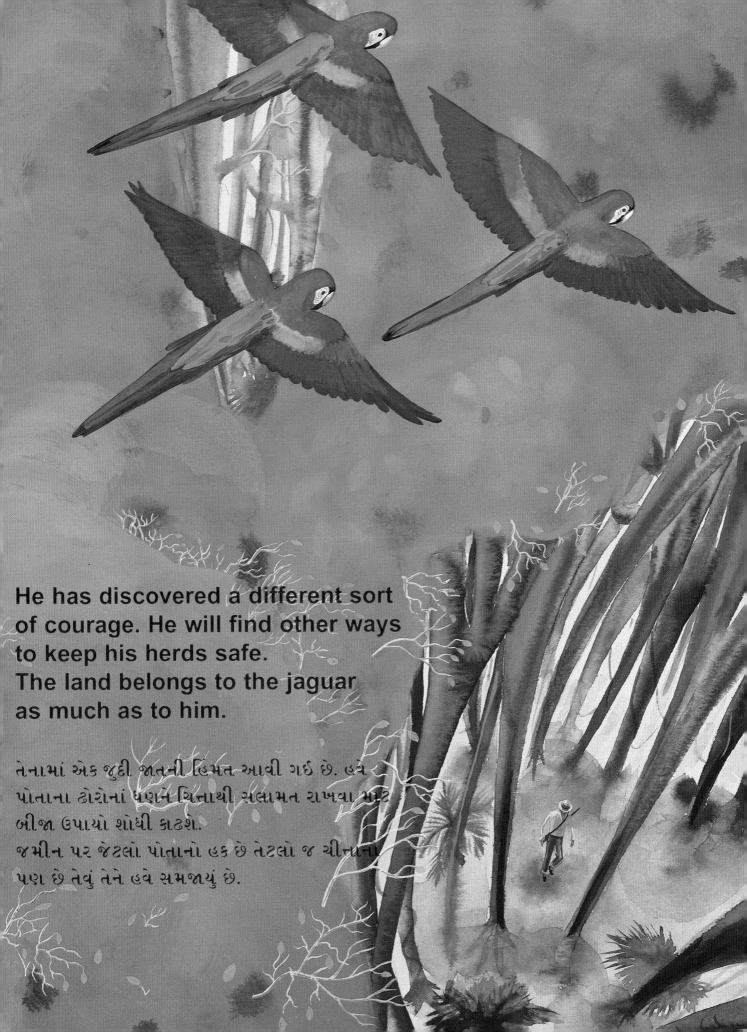

He has discovered a different sort
of courage. He will find other ways
to keep his herds safe.
The land belongs to the jaguar
as much as to him.

તેનામાં એક જુદી જાતની હિંમત આવી ગઈ છે. હવે
પોતાના ઢોરોનાં ધણને ચિંતાથી સલામત રાખવા માટે
બીજા ઉપાયો શોધી કાઢશે.
જમીન પર જેટલો પોતાનો હક છે તેટલો જ ચીત્તાનો
પણ છે તેવું તેને હવે સમજાયું છે.

More About Jaguar

WHY WAS HOWLER MONKEY SO FRIGHTENED?

• All animals fear the jaguar, but howler monkeys have an especially deep fear.

• Sometimes a howler monkey becomes a willing victim. It seems to give up all thought of escape and as if impelled by an invisible force, cries out with alarm and is drawn towards the jaguar!

WHAT ABOUT PIRANHAS, CAIMANS AND ANACONDAS?

• Piranhas are aggressive fish. They always attack in groups, sometimes hundreds at a time. Some jaguars have lost as much as 15cm of their tail to piranhas!

• Spectacled caimans are related more to alligators than crocodiles. They do not attack humans and their main predators are anacondas and jaguars.

• Anacondas always live near water where they like to submerge themselves. An anaconda will lash out, coiling around unsuspecting prey until the victim suffocates.

• This snake digests slowly and after one good-sized meal can survive many months without food.

• It is the largest snake in the world (not the longest, but the most bulky), measuring 5-6 metres and weighing 150kg.

• A fully grown anaconda is dangerous to man and even to a jaguar!

WHY IS JAGUAR SO POWERFUL?

• From Central America as far south as Argentina, Jaguar is at the top of the food chain. This means he has no natural predator apart from man.

• He is the third largest of the world's big cats, reaching 50-100kg in weight.

• His jaw is the most powerful, relative to size, of all the big cats. He can bite straight through the armour-plated shell of a large turtle.

WHAT DOES 'THE RAGING SPIRIT JAGUAR' MEAN TO THE HUNTER?

• Throughout the tropical forests and plains of Central and South America, there is a fear of the jaguar, bordering on worship.

• Although the jaguar is rarely seen, its tracks are often visible, and its roar sounds at night, giving a feeling of menacing presence.

• The jaguar is respected for its physical powers, but belief in its supernatural power is very important too.

• The hunter, in this book, has known a sorcerer who transformed himself into a jaguar.

He has also heard of the forest
Indians' initiation rites, during which
a boy passes into manhood and
sees his 'Spirit Master'. What he
sees is important knowledge and
must be kept secret.

For some, the 'Spirit Master' is an
eagle, for some a snake, for others
a jaguar.

When a boy knows his 'Spirit
Master' is a jaguar, he knows too
that his soul has 'jaguar' qualities.
He is quick-witted, cunning and
strong. And afterwards in the forest,
he watches out for the jaguar; for
to harm him would be to endanger
his own soul.

The hunter will have heard many
stories of such power. He may only
half believe them, but nonetheless
they affect him.

So when the 'raging jaguar spirit'
confronts him, he is both awestruck
and afraid.

WHY WOULD A JAGUAR KILL CATTLE?

A jaguar may roam into new territory where favourite prey, peccary and
deer, have been over-hunted by man.
If there is a road nearby, this is
likely. So the jaguar is forced to risk
endangering itself by coming closer
to man, and taking livestock.

If a jaguar is old or if it has been
wounded in the past, (gun-shot
damage to the jaw, for example),
then it will not be fit enough to
hunt wild prey.

WHY IS THE JAGUAR AN ENDANGERED SPECIES?

• Up until 1970, when the jaguar
was officially listed as an
endangered species, many
thousands were killed for their fur.
During the last 3 years before the
ban, 30,000 skins were imported
into the USA alone!
• Since such trade was made illegal,
the threat now comes from the
jaguar's shrinking habitat.

WHAT DOES THE FUTURE HOLD?

• The pressure on wilderness from
increasing human population is a
big problem, especially for the
jaguar. Because each jaguar needs a
territory of 65 square km in which
to roam, there must be very large
wild areas left, where jaguars can
live and breed.
• One idea is to have large nature
reserves connected by smaller areas
of wilderness, within which wild
creatures can take cover whilst
passing from one reserve to
another. These are known as
'wilderness corridors'.
• Another idea is to relocate the
few jaguars that become
accustomed to preying on cattle.
• In Venezuela, a few enlightened
cattle ranchers use the combination
of wildlife corridors, undisturbed
forest and managed pastureland
so that cattle, wildlife and
eco-tourism can co-exist.

HOW TO FIND OUT MORE:

LIVING EARTH
Warwick House
106 Harrow Road
London W2 1XD
England

WILDLIFE CONSERVATION SOCIETY
2300 Southern
Boulevard
Bronx
New York 10460
USA

RAINFOREST ACTION NETWORK
450 Sansome
Suite 700
San Francisco
California 94111
USA

W.W.F (U.K.)
Panda House
Weyside Park
Godalming
Surrey
GU7 1XR
England

1. IGUANA
2. GREAT EGRET
3. SCARLET IBIS
4. CRESTED CARACARA
5. BOAT-BILLED HERON
6. RUFOUS-VENTED CHACHALACA
7. SIDENECK TURTLE
8. YELLOW-KNOBBED CURRASOW
9. CRAB-EATING FOX
10. HOATZIN
11. BLUE MORPHO BUTTERFLY
12. CAPYBARA
13. JABIRU STORK
14. WHITE-TAILED DEER

The Story of *Jaguar*

• *Jaguar* is set in the Venezuelan Llanos, which lies noth of the great River Orinoco. In the rainy season, much of it becomes floodplain. In *Jaguar*, it is the dry season.

• In the Llanos, live the Llaneros (cowboys), very skilled horsemen who are used to working in extreme conditions. They work throughout floods, fires, and drought, riding for many hours each day under the intense tropical sun. Often as they ride, they sing songs of their lives on the plains . . . of horses and cattle, of women and romance, and of the beauty of nature, which they see all around them.

GARY HODGES

• Their ancestors were either indigenous Indians or Africans or Spaniards. Now their descendants, a mixture of all three races, are justly proud to be Llaneros.

• In 1992, Helen Cowcher joined a group of British and Venezuelan artists to paint the richly diverse habitats of Venezuela. The resulting group exhibition in Caracas raised funds for environmental education.

• Helen Cowcher stayed at HATO PIÑERO in the northern Llanos. This cattle ranch is world famous for its flora and fauna and prides itself in being a model of sustainable development. Helen has returned many times drawn back by the land, the people and the wildlife.

Helen with Gertrudis "a Llanero who can see a tiny humming bird, even when it's behind him!"

THANK YOU to:
Señor Antonio Julio Branger,
FUNDACIÓN BRANGER
and all at the Biological Station,
Hato Piñero, Ana Jesus,
José Gertrudis Gamarra
and all the other friends in Venezuela,
who have helped me:
LIVING EARTH, TIERRA VIVA
and the BRITISH COUNCIL.